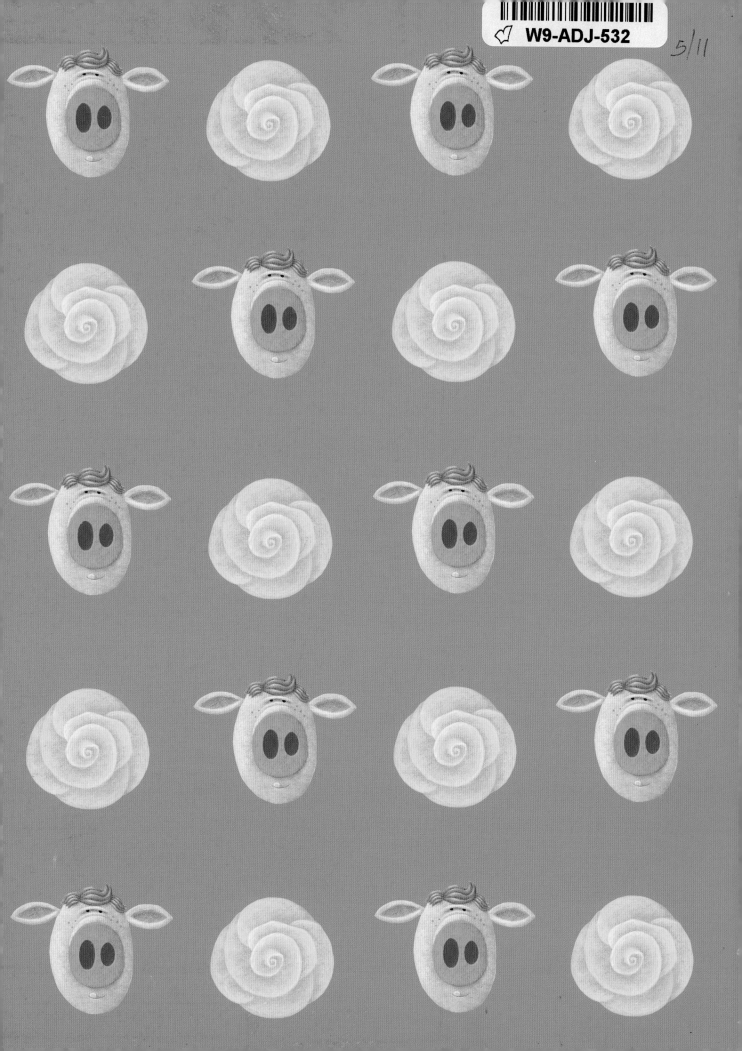

5/11

DESERT ROSE
and Her Highfalutin Hog

Alison Jackson

illustrated by

Keith Graves

 Walker & Company
New York

First published in the United States of America in 2009
by Walker Publishing Company, Inc.
Visit Walker & Company's Web site at www.walkeryoungreaders.com

For information about permission to reproduce selections from this book,
write to Permissions, Walker & Company, 175 Fifth Avenue, New York,
New York 10010

Library of Congress Cataloging-in-Publication Data
Jackson, Alison.
Desert Rose and her highfalutin hog / Alison Jackson ;
illustrated by Keith Graves.
    p.   cm.
Summary: Upon finding a large gold nugget on her pig farm,
Desert Rose sets out to buy the biggest, fattest hog in Texas to
enter in the state fair, but first she must get the hog to Laredo
and every animal she asks for help is just as "ornery" as the hog.
ISBN-13: 978-0-8027-9833-6 • ISBN-10: 0-8027-9833-0
(hardcover)
ISBN-13: 978-0-8027-9834-3 • ISBN-10: 0-8027-9834-9
(reinforced)
[1. Tall tales. 2. Animals—Fiction. 3. Texas—Fiction.]
I. Graves, Keith, ill. II. Title.
PZ7.J13217Des 2009   [E]—dc22   2009000206

Art created with acrylic paint on illustration board
Typeset in Highlander
Book design by Nicole Gastonguay

Printed in China by SNP Leefung Printers Limited
(hardcover) 10 9 8 7 6 5 4 3 2 1
(reinforced) 10 9 8 7 6 5 4 3 2 1

All papers used by Walker & Company are natural, recyclable
products made from wood grown in well-managed forests.
The manufacturing processes conform to the environmental
regulations of the country of origin.

Out yonder, where the scalding Texas sun meets the Guadalupe Mountains, there once lived a gritty pig farmer by the name of Desert Rose.

Desert Rose was fixin' to muck out the pig stalls one day, when she came upon a solid gold nugget just a-lyin' there in the mud.

"Hot butter beans!" Rose exclaimed. "I'll mosey on into town with this here gold nugget and buy me the biggest, fattest hog in all of Texas. Then I can win first prize at the state fair in Laredo!"

When she got to town, Desert Rose did indeed pick out the biggest, fattest hog in all of Texas. And she gladly parted with her shiny gold nugget.

In her hurry to get to the fair, Rose decided to take a shortcut.

She soon came upon a bubbling creek. But her hog would not set one hoof in that gurgling water.

Desert Rose sat down and thought for a moment. Then she had herself a fine notion.

"Hog! Hog! Drink up all the water! Or I'll miss the state fair in Laredo."

"Ain't thirsty," huffed the hog, stubborn as a Texas mule. And he plopped himself down on the bank.

"Well, *tickle my tail feathers!*" cried Desert Rose. "You are one highfalutin hog!"

Rose took a gander round and spied a coyote a-sleepin'
in the shade.

"Coyote! Coyote! Nip that hog! Hog won't drink water,
and I'll miss the state fair in Laredo."

"Too tired," complained the coyote.

"Well, *bite my boots*!" cried Desert Rose. "You are
one coldhearted coyote!"

Rose sifted through the sand and spied a snake rattlin' its way down a long, slender hole.

"Snake! Snake! Wake that coyote! Coyote won't nip hog, hog won't drink water, and I'll miss the state fair in Laredo."

"Too hot," snapped the snake.

"Well, *bust my breeches!*" cried Desert Rose. "You are one persnickety snake!"

Rose searched high and low, then spied a cowboy a-ridin' and a-rompin' in his neckerchief and spurs.

"Cowboy! Cowboy! Spur that snake! Snake won't wake coyote, coyote won't nip hog, hog won't drink water, and I'll miss the state fair in Laredo."

"'Fraid of snakes," countered the cowboy.

"Well, *starch my stirrups!*" cried Desert Rose. "You are one contrary cowboy!"

Rose studied the cowboy's bronco a-saggin' and a-sinkin' under his saddle.

"Bronco! Bronco! Buck that cowboy! Cowboy won't spur snake, snake won't wake coyote, coyote won't nip hog, hog won't drink water, and I'll miss the state fair in Laredo."

"Bad back!" bellowed the bronco.

"Well, *chop my chaps*!" cried Desert Rose. "You are one bothersome bronco!"

Rose scoured the skyline and spied a genuine Texas longhorn steer lyin' lazy-like in the black-eyed Susans.

"Longhorn! Longhorn! Chase that bronco! Bronco won't buck cowboy, cowboy won't spur snake, snake won't wake coyote, coyote won't nip hog, hog won't drink water, and I'll miss the state fair in Laredo."

"Lame leg," lamented the longhorn.

"Well, *pickle my pistols!*" cried Desert Rose. "You are one lethargic longhorn!"

Rose surveyed the desert and spied a mangy armadillo movin' just as slow as you please through a crusty crop of cacti.

This partic'lar armadillo was chock-full of nothing but mean armadillo attitude.

Well.

After all that had passed, what did Desert Rose have to lose?

Looking that armored beast right in the eye, she said, "Mr. Armadillo, sir, I'm plumb tuckered out. Won't you *please* dig under that longhorn? Longhorn won't chase bronco, bronco won't buck cowboy, cowboy won't spur snake, snake won't wake coyote, coyote won't nip hog, hog won't drink water, and I'll miss the state fair in Laredo."

The armadillo blinked at Desert Rose.

"What's in it for me?" he drawled.

Now, Desert Rose hadn't been fixin' to give *anything* to the greedy varmint. But at last she answered, "If my hog wins first prize, I'll bring back two hundred pounds of ants, beetles, and grubs fer ya, cross my heart."

The armadillo tipped his narrow head at Rose.

"I reckon I can dig under that longhorn a spell," he said.

And with those words, the armadillo began to dig under

the longhorn . . .

The longhorn began to chase the bronco . . .

The bronco began to buck the cowboy . . .

The cowboy began to spur the snake . . .

The snake began to wake the coyote . . .

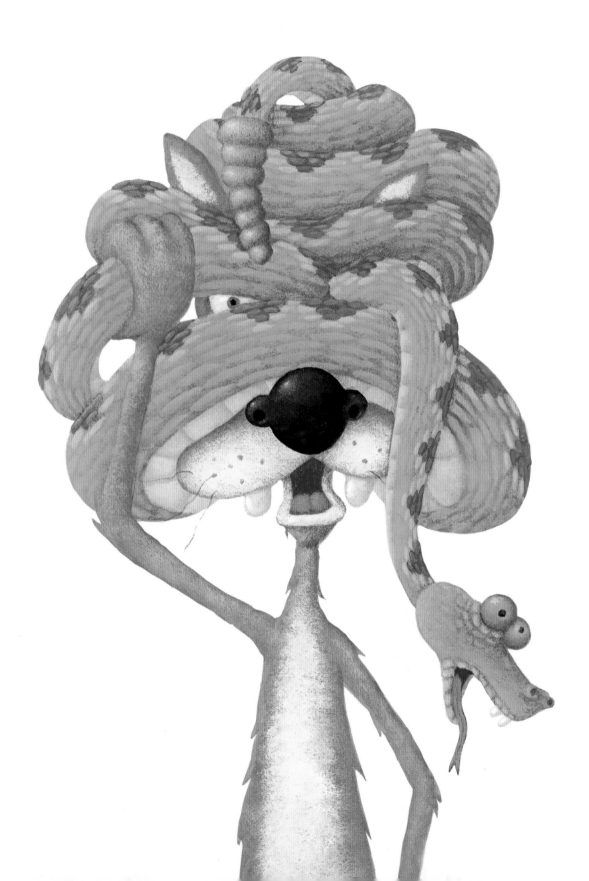

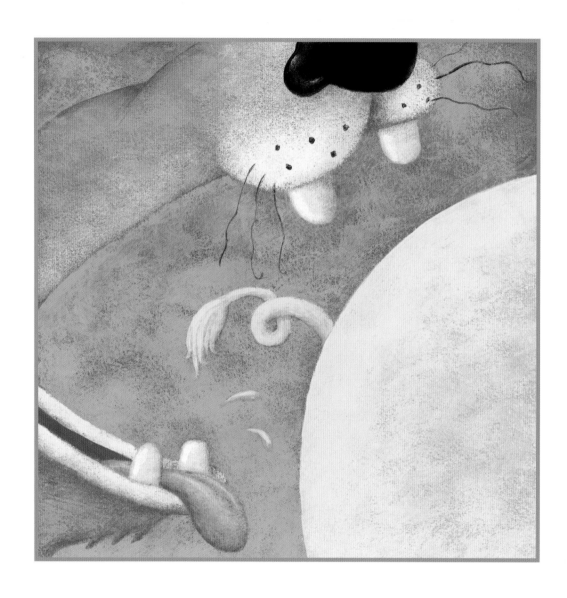

The coyote began to nip the hog . . .

. . . and the hog drank up all the water in that
bubbling creek.

    "Hoooooooeeeeeey!" whooped Desert Rose.
"You are one thirsty hog!"

Then the whole lot of them set off, with Desert Rose leadin' the pack. And they made it to the state fair in Laredo with only minutes to spare.

Sure enough, that highfalutin hog won first prize at the fair.

And true to her promise, Rose hauled back a
Texas-size helping of ants, beetles, and grubs.
Two hundred pounds of them!

But every year when it comes time to take her
prize-winning hog to the state fair in Laredo,
Rose always takes the *long* road out of town.
Just in case.